Pacific Insurance Union

## Book of Rates

San Francisco - for the use and guidance of fire underwriters on the Pacific

Coast

Pacific Insurance Union

**Book of Rates**
*San Francisco - for the use and guidance of fire underwriters on the Pacific Coast*

ISBN/EAN: 9783337255589

Printed in Europe, USA, Canada, Australia, Japan

Cover: Foto ©Andreas Hilbeck / pixelio.de

More available books at **www.hansebooks.com**

FOR THE USE AND GUIDANCE OF

# FIRE UNDERWRITERS

ON THE

## PACIFIC COAST.

SAN FRANCISCO:

PUBLISHED BY THE PACIFIC INSURANCE UNION

II. S. CROCKER & CO., PRINTERS.

*February, 1887.*

# INDEX.

# Rule for Determining Rate of Premium.

First ascertain the classification of the building to be insured, or containing the property to be insured, as per the "Classification of Buildings," on page 5, designated B, C and D. It being ascertained which of these classes the building belongs to, refer to the "Alphabetical Table of Hazards," pages 7 to 23 inclusive, and the highest rate named therein for any occupancy† in the building (*not prefixed with a star* \*), will be the *basis rate* for such building, and all contents thereof not prefixed with a star\*.

Such occupancies as are prefixed with a star\* take their own *basis rate*, unless such rate is less than the *basis rate* of the highest rated occupancy not prefixed with a star\*, in which latter case such highest rated occupancy determines the *basis rate* for the entire building and contents, excepting higher rated star\* hazards.

When a building does not contain any of the occupancies named in the "Alphabetical Table of Hazards," or when all of the occupancies are prefixed by a star\*, the *basis rate* for such building shall be that of its class, B, C or D, given under the head of "Classification of Buildings," on page 5; and the *basis rate* for each star\* occupancy contained in such building shall be taken from the "Alphabetical Table of Hazards."

The *basis rate* being correctly ascertained, next refer to the rules concerning additions for deficiencies, privileges and exposures, on pages 24 to 31 inclusive, and the proper charges therefor (if any are to be made), added to the *basis rate*, fix the minimum tariff rate for any given risk, *except* in the cases where the rate thus ascertained exceeds the maximum rate given on page 31.

† If a building is not occupied, the evident purpose for which it has been or is being constructed, or for which it is to be occupied, shall determine its occupancy.

NOTE.—In connection with the above rule, see General Rules 2, page 32, and 7 page 34.

\* STAR HAZARDS.—The stars prefixed to stocks in the schedule do not apply to the furniture of the store containing the stock.

When a building contains only star hazards and occupancies (such as Dwellings) having lower basis rates than the building, according to its class, the basis rate for such building, and for such occupancies, other than the star hazards, shall be that of its class as per Classification of Buildings, page 5.

# Classification of Buildings.

## B CLASS.

A building with all of its exterior walls built of brick, stone, adobe or concrete, and having a metal, slate, tile, brick or composition roof, and side walls extending above the roof. A building with side walls not extending above the roof, but in all other particulars up to the standard of B Class, may be rated as such if detached 50 feet from all B, C or D Class buildings.

NOTE.—That any roof, other than a wooden roof, shall be considered as meeting the above requirements of a B Class building in respect to roofs, even if such roof is protected by a wooden roof.

†*Basis rate* on a building of this class ...................... 1.00

## C CLASS.

A building which varies from the standard of a B Class building in any one or more of the following particulars, viz:

*First.*—In being constructed of iron,
*Second.*—In having a front wall (only) of wood.
*Third.*—In having a shingle, shake or mansard roof.
*Fourth.*—In having side walls not extending above the roof, unless the building is detached 50 feet from all other B, C or D Class Buildings.
*Fifth.*—In having a frame structure on the roof, as described in Rule 3 on page 32.

†*Basis rate* on a building of this class ...................... 1.20

The several divisions of a B or C Class building shall not be considered as distinct buildings, although separated from each other by a brick or stone wall or walls, unless such wall or walls are without an opening or openings, and rise above the roof. Any number of divisions constitute one building, when the division wall or walls do not rise above the roof, and the rate for the highest rated occupancy in such a building (not prefixed in the Table of Hazards with a *) is the *basis rate* for the building.

Two or more distinct B and (or) C Class buildings immediately adjoining and connected with each other by an opening or openings shall be considered (as to rate) as constituting one building, unless each of such openings is provided with a wooden door two inches in thickness and covered with tin or galvanized iron, or with an iron door at least three-sixteenths of an inch in thickness; and the rate for the highest rated occupancy in the buildings (not prefixed in the Table of Hazards with a *) is the *basis rate* for the buildings.

## D CLASS.

A frame building, or a building partly constructed of brick, stone, iron, adobe or concrete, but not up to the standard of a C Class building.

†*Basis rate* on a building of this class ...................... 1.50

☞ The foregoing rates apply to buildings and their contents for which there is no rate in the following "Alphabetical Table of Hazards," and to buildings containing only star (*) hazards.

[* Book San Fran.—1.]

# Alphabetical Table of Hazards.

## YEARLY BASIS RATES FOR $100.

The *basis rate* for **C Class** is one-fifth more than **B Class** rate.
(See rule 21, page 39.)

|  | B Class. | D Class. |
|---|---|---|
| ACADEMIES, day students only ‖ | .75 | 1.25 |
| Academies, boarding, with dormitories ‖ | .90 | 1.50 |
| Agricultural Implement Stocks | 1.25 | 1.75 |
| Agricultural Implement Factories, hand power | 2.00 | 3.00 |
| Agricultural Implement Factories, steam power † | 2.50 | 4.00 |
| Ale and or Beer Stocks, wholesale (no saloon or bar) | 1.00 | 1.50 |
| Alms or County Poor Houses ‖ | 1.25 | 2.00 |
| *Apothecaries' Stocks, retail (see Drug Stocks) | 1.50 | 2.25 |
| Asphaltum Roofing Establishments | 4.00 | 7.00 |
| Assaying and Refining Establishments | 1.50 | 2.00 |
| Asylums, Blind, Deaf and Dumb, and Orphan ‖ | 1.00 | 1.75 |
| Asylums, Insane ‖ | 1.25 | 2.00 |
| Auction and Commission Stocks, wholesale | 1.00 | 1.75 |
| Auction Stores, retail | 1.50 | 2.50 |
| Awnings, (see rule 4, page 32) | | |
| ............................ | | |
| BAG (sewed) FACTORIES (no steam power) | 1.25 | 2.00 |
| Bag (sewed) Factories, steam power † | 1.75 | 3.00 |
| Bag (paper) Factories, steam power † | 1.50 | 2.50 |
| Bakeries (no steam power) | 1.50 | 2.25 |
| Bakeries, steam power (to be specially rated) | | |

The *basis rate* for C Class is one-fifth more than B Class.
†The charge for Steam Boiler or Steam Power is included.
‖See rule for Long Term Risks on page 35.

| | B Class. | D Class. |
|---|---|---|
| *Bakers' Stocks (no oven)................ | 1.25 | 2.00 |
| Banking Houses, Furniture and Fixtures therein........................... | 1.00 | 1.50 |
| Barbers' Shops, Furniture, Fix. and Stocks. | 1.25 | 2.00 |
| Bark and or Bark Sheds...................... | | 1.50 |
| Barns, private, within the corporate limits of towns ‖........................... | .75 | 1.00 |
| Barns, private, outside of corporate limits of towns ‖. If located within 100 yards of dwelling upon same premises on which barn is located..................... | | |
| Barns, private, outside the corporate limits of towns ‖............................ | | |
| Barrel Factories, Steam Power †.......... | 3.50 | 5.00 |
| Basket and Willow Ware Factories....... | 1.40 | 2.25 |
| Basket and Willow Ware Stocks.......... | 1.25 | 2.00 |
| Bath Houses (no charge for boiler)....... | 1.25 | 2.00 |
| Bell Hangers' Shops.................... | 1.25 | 2.00 |
| Billiard Saloons....................... | 1.25 | 1.75 |
| Billiard Saloons in Hotels (see rule 6, p. 33) | 1.50 | 2.75 |
| Billiard Table Factories................. | 3.00 | 4.25 |
| Blacksmiths' and or Horse Shoeing Shops...... | 1.25 | 2.00 |
| Blacksmiths' and Wheelwrights' Shops..... | 2.00 | 3.00 |
| Bleaching Shops (Straw, etc.) †.......... | 1.65 | 2.75 |
| Blind, Sash and Door Factories, hand power | 3.25 | 4.50 |
| Blind, Sash and Door Factories, water power | 4.00 | 6.00 |
| Blind, Sash and Door Factories, steam power† | 6.00 | 9.00 |
| Blind, Sash and Door Stocks............. | 1.50 | 2.50 |
| Block and or Pump Factories................ | 2.00 | 3.00 |
| Boarding and or Lodging Houses (see rule 17, page 36)......................... | | |
| Containing 10 sleeping rooms.......... | .85 | 1.25 |
| Exceeding 10, and not exceeding 15 sleeping rooms ........................ | 1.00 | 1.50 |
| Exceeding 15, and not exceeding 20 sleeping rooms ........................ | 1.10 | 1.75 |
| Exceeding 20 sleeping rooms.......... | 1.25 | 2.00 |
| Boat Building Shops................... | 2.25 | 3.50 |
| Boats (steam) on stocks and laid up.......... | | 2.00 |

The *basis rate* for C Class is one-fifth more than B Class.
†The charge for Steam Boiler or Steam Power is included.
‖See rule for Long Term Risks on page 35.

| | |
|---|---|
| Boats (steam) running.............. | |
| Boiler Shops†.................. | |
| Book Binderies................. | |
| *Book and Stationery Stocks......... | 3.10 |
| Boot and Shoe Factories (see rule 23, | 5.50 |
| Boot and Shoe Stocks, wholesale..... | 1.50 |
| Boot and Shoe Shops and Stocks, work and retail sales only (rubber may be used during daylight only)... | 1.65 |
| Bottling Establishments............. | 2.00 |
| Bowling Alleys................. | 2.00 |
| Box Factories, steam power†........ | 9.00 |
| Breweries (to be specially rated)..... | |
| Brewers' Stocks................. | 2.00 |
| Bridges, foot and carriage, free or toll‖. | 1.25 |
| Bridges, railroad, open ‖........... | 1.75 |
| Bridges, railroad, covered ‖......... | 2.00 |
| Broom and Brush Factories........ | 3.75 |
| Broom Factories................ | 3.75 |
| Brush Factories................ | 3.50 |
| Broom Corn in bales.............. | 2.25 |
| Broom Corn, loose.............. | 2.75 |
| Bucket, Pail and Tub Factories, dry detached as per Tables of Exposures† | 8.00 |
| Bucket, Pail and Tub Factories, dry not detached†................ | 9.00 |
| Butchers' Shops, without rendering kettle | 1.50 |
| Butchers' Shops, with rendering kettle.. | 2.25 |
| Butchers' Shops (rendering and smoking | 2.75 |
| Butter and Cheese Stocks.......... | 1.50 |
| | |
| | |
| CABINET SHOPS............. | 3.50 |
| Candle Factories (see Soap and Candle Factories) ............... | |

The basis rate for C Class is one-fifth more than
†The charge for Steam Boiler or Steam Power
‖See rule for Long Term Risks on page 36.

| | B Class. | D Class. |
|---|---|---|
| Candy <sup>and</sup><sub>or</sub> Confectionery Factories......... | 1.50 | 2.25 |
| *Candy <sup>and</sup><sub>or</sub> Confectionery Stocks (no manufacturing)...................... | 1.25 | 2.00 |
| Canned Fish, Fruit, Meat and Vegetables Stocks (no manufacturing)............ | 1.00 | 1.75 |
| Cap Factories (see Hat and Cap Factories). | 1.25 | 2.00 |
| Carpenters' Risk (see rules 8 and 9, page 34, and rule 16, page 36)................ | | |
| Carpenters' Shops...................... | 2.25 | 3.50 |
| Carpet Stocks........................ | 1.00 | 1.50 |
| Carriage Trimming Shops (no woodworking)................................ | 1.75 | 2.75 |
| Carriage and Wagon Repositories, for finishing Stock........................... | 1.25 | 2.00 |
| Carriage, Wagon and Car Factories (no power) ........................... | 2.00 | 3.00 |
| Carriage, Wagon and Car Factory, steam power †..................... | 2.50 | 4.00 |
| Cement Stocks, without lime (see Lime)..... | 1.00 | 1.50 |
| Chair Stocks (setting up done)........... | 1.50 | 2.50 |
| Cheese and Butter Stocks................ | 1.00 | 1.50 |
| Cheese Factories..................... | 1.25 | 2.00 |
| Chemical Laboratories.................. | 2.50 | 3.50 |
| Chiccory Factories and Kilns †........... | 3.75 | 6.00 |
| Chinese Merchandise (see rule 30, page 42) | 1.50 | 2.50 |
| Chinese Wash <sup>and</sup><sub>or</sub> Ironing Houses........ | 1.75 | 3.00 |
| Churches ‖ (see Frescoed Work, etc.)...... | .75 | 1.00 |
| *Cigar Factories ..................... | 2.00 | 3.00 |
| *Cigar and Tobacco Stocks, wholesale...... | 1.25 | 2.00 |
| *Cigar and Tobacco Stocks, retail (see rule 6, page 33)........................ | 1.50 | 2.25 |
| City Halls, with or without jail ‖.......... | 1.00 | 1.75 |
| City Jails ‖............................ | 1.00 | 1.75 |
| Cloak and Mantilla Stocks.............. | 1.25 | 2.00 |
| *Clock Stocks........................ | 1.25 | 1.75 |
| Clothing Factories..................... | 1.25 | 2.00 |
| Clothing Stocks (ready-made) <sup>and</sup><sub>or</sub> Cloth..... | 1.00 | 1.50 |
| Clothing Stocks, second hand............ | 1.25 | 2.00 |
| Club Rooms.......................... | 1.25 | 2.00 |

The *basis rate* for C Class is one-fifth more than B Class.
†The charge for Steam Boiler or Steam Power is included.
‖See rule for Long Term Risks on page 35.

|  | B Class. | D Class. |
|---|---|---|
| Coal Oil and similar Stock, sold exclusively or with Lamp Stocks (see rule 19, page 37) | 2.00 | 3.00 |
| Coal and or Wood Yards (see rules 6, page 33, and 7, page 34) .................... | | 1.75 |
| Cobblers' Shops (see rule 2, page 32)...... | | |
| Coffee and or Spice Mills† ................... | 2.75 | 4.00 |
| *Coffee and Spice Stocks (no roasting)..... | 1.25 | 2.00 |
| Coffin-makers' Shops .................... | 2.25 | 3.50 |
| Colleges, without dormitories‖ ............ | .75 | 1.25 |
| Colleges, with dormitories‖ .............. | .90 | 1.50 |
| Composition Roofing Works ............. | 4.00 | 7.00 |
| Coopers' Shops, hand power............. | 2.25 | 3.50 |
| Coopers' Shops, steam power† ........... | 3.50 | 5.00 |
| Coppersmiths' Shops.................... | 1.50 | 2.50 |
| Cordage and Rope Stocks............... | 1.25 | 2.00 |
| *Cork Stocks......................... | 1.10 | 1.85 |
| *Costumers' Stocks..................... | 1.50 | 2.25 |
| Cotton Mills (to be specially rated)....... | | |
| County Jails‖........................ | 1.00 | 1.75 |
| County Offices‖....................... | 1.00 | 1.75 |
| County Poor Houses ‖ .................. | 1.25 | 2.00 |
| Court Houses, with or without jail‖....... | 1.00 | 1.75 |
| Crockery, China and Glassware.......... | 1.35 | 2.10 |
| Curriers' and Leather Dressers' Shops (no tanning, or bark mill) .............. | 1.50 | 2.50 |
| .................................... | | |
| DAIRIES............................ | 1.00 | 1.25 |
| Dentists' and or Doctors' Offices (see rule 2, page 32) ................................ | | |
| *Dentists' Stocks in stores............... | 1.25 | 2.00 |
| Depots, railroad, freight or passenger...... | 1.50 | 2.50 |
| Distilleries † ........................... | 6.00 | 9.00 |
| Dormitories, Academy, College and Seminary‖ | .90 | 1.50 |
| Dressmakers' Workrooms (see rule 2, p. 32) | | |
| Drill Halls and Armories................ | 1.25 | 2.00 |
| Druggists' Glass Stocks ................. | 1.35 | 2.10 |
| *Drug Stores, retail.................... | 1.50 | 2.25 |

The *basis rate* for C Class is one–fifth more than B Class.
†The charge for Steam Boiler or Steam Power is included.
‖See rule for Long Term Risks on page 35.

|  | B Class. | D Class. |
|---|---|---|
| Drug Stores, wholesale (no manufacturing by fire heat)............................ | 1.75 | 2.50 |
| Drug stores, wholesale, where compounding or manufacturing by fire heat .......... | 2.00 | 2.75 |
| Dry Goods Stocks, wholesale............. | 1.00 | 1.50 |
| Dry Goods Stocks, retail................ | 1.10 | 1.65 |
| Dwellings ‖ (see rule 1, page 32; also see Frescoed Work, etc)...(C Class, 55 cts.) | .50 | .60 |
| Dyeing and Cleaning Establishments†..... | 1.75 | 2.75 |
| ...................... | ...... | ...... |
| *Earthenware Stocks............... | 1.25 | 2.00 |
| Elevators, Grain (to be specially rated).... |  |  |
| Engine Houses, Fire‖................. | 1.00 | 1.50 |
| Express Offices, Furniture and Fixtures... | 1.10 | 1.85 |
| ...................... | ...... | ...... |
| Fair and Race Ground Amphitheatres and Buildings ........................ |  | 3.00 |
| *Fancy Goods and Variety Stocks........ | 1.35 | 2.00 |
| Feed Mills (no flour made), steam power†.. | 1.25 | 2.00 |
| Feed Stores, without hay or straw........ | 1.00 | 1.50 |
| Feed Stores, with hay or straw.......... | 2.00 | 3.50 |
| Fences of wood‖..................... |  | 1.25 |
| Findings (Boot and Shoe) and Leather.... | 1.25 | 1.75 |
| Fire-proof Cellars, inside of frame buildings, Stocks in (no addition for exposure)..... |  |  |

NOTE.—*Stocks in such cellars outside of buildings take rate according to their contents with no addition for exposures.*
For the purpose of rating, such cellars may be regarded as B Class buildings.

| Firework Stocks...................... | 2.00 | 3.00 |
|---|---|---|
| Fireworks. Privilege to keep on sale...... |  |  |

NOTE.—*For the privilege of keeping Fireworks on sale, a charge of one-half of one per cent additional premium shall be made for each month or portion of a month. (See rule 16, page 36.)*

| Flax in bales........................ | 1.50 | 2.50 |
|---|---|---|
| Flaxseed............................ | 1.00 | 1.60 |

The *basis rate* for C Class is one-fifth more than B Class.
†The charge for Steam Boiler or Steam power is included.
‖See rule for Long Term Risks, on page 35.

| | B Class. | D Class. |
|---|---|---|
| Flour Mills, water power................ | 2.75 | 4.00 |
| Flour Mills, steam power†.............. | 4.00 | 5.50 |
| Foundries, Brass† (see rule 31, page 42)... | 2.00 | 3.00 |
| Foundries, Iron, without pattern shops†.... | 2.00 | 3.50 |
| Foundries, Iron, with pattern shops† (see rule 31, page 42).................... | 2.50 | 4.25 |
| Frescoed Work.................................... | | |
| NOTE.—*For Frescoed Work or Gilding on Walls or Ceilings, charge 25 cents more than the rate of the building.* | | |
| Fringe and Trimming Factories.......... | 1.50 | 2.50 |
| *Fringe and Trimming Stocks............ | 1.35 | 2.00 |
| Fruit Canning Establishments† (see rule 26, page 40)........................ | 1.70 | 3.00 |
| Fruit Drying Establishments............ | 2.50 | 4.00 |
| *Fruit Stocks, wholesale................ | 1.25 | 1.75 |
| *Fruit Stores, retail.................... | 1.35 | 2.00 |
| *Fur Stocks............................ | 1.25 | 2.00 |
| Furniture Factories, hand power......... | 3.50 | 5.00 |
| Furniture Factories, steam power †....... | 6.00 | 9.00 |
| Furniture Stocks (no upholstering, manufacturing or setting up done in the building). | 1.50 | 2.50 |
| Furniture Stocks, where upholstering or setting up is done...................... | 1.75 | 2.75 |
| Furniture Stocks, second-hand ......... | 1.75 | 2.75 |
| | | |
| GAS FIXTURE STOCKS.................... | 1.25 | 2.00 |
| Gas Works........................... | 2.50 | 3.50 |
| General Merchandise (see rule 22, page 39). | 1.25 | 1.75 |
| *Gentlemen's Furnishing Goods.......... | 1.25 | 1.75 |
| Glass Stocks (window and or plate)........... | 1.35 | 2.10 |
| *Glove Factories...................... | 1.25 | 2.00 |
| Glue Factories, with steam power †....... | 2.25 | 3.50 |
| Gold Beaters' Factories................ | 1.25 | 2.00 |
| Grain (cut, uncut, in stacks or in sacks, while in the field) .... | | 5.00 |
| NOTE.—Policies covering grain in field may be transferred to cover same grain in warehouse for balance of term of such policies; but *no return premium can be paid on account of lower rates.* | | |
| Granaries, private.................... | .90 | 1.25 |
| NOTE.—*A private granary is to be understood to be a farm building used exclusively by the farmer for the storage or keeping of his own grain, and other farm products, exclusive of hay, straw, broom corn, and unbaled hops; also exclusive of farm implements.* | | |

The *basis rate* for C Class is one-fifth more than B Class.
†The charge for Steam Boiler or Steam Power is included.
‖See rule for Long Term Risks on page 35.　　　[Book San Fran.—2.]

| | B Class. | D Class. |
|---|---|---|
| Grocery Stocks, wholesale................ | 1.00 | 1.50 |
| Grocery Stocks, retail................. | 1.00 | 1.50 |
| Gunny Cloth, and Bag Stocks........... | 1.00 | 1.50 |
| Gunsmiths' Shops and Stocks........... | 1.35 | 2.10 |
| Gymnasiums................ | 1.25 | 2.00 |
| ................................ | ............ | |
| *HAIR (human) STOCKS............... | 1.50 | 2.50 |
| Halls, Masons', Odd Fellows' and other Societies (see Frescoed Work)............ | 1.25 | 1.75 |
| Halls, Public, without scenery (see Frescoed Work)...................... | 1.35 | 2.00 |
| Halls, Public, with scenery (see Frescoed Work)...................... | 2.25 | 3.50 |
| *Hardware and Cutlery Stock........... | 1.10 | 1.65 |
| Hardwood Lumber Stocks............... | 1.00 | 1.50 |
| Harness and Saddle Factories (no collar making)..... | 1.50 | 2.50 |
| Harness and Saddle Factories (with collar making)..... | 2.00 | 3.00 |
| *Harness and Saddle Stocks wholesale..... | 1.25 | 1.75 |
| *Harness and Saddle Stocks (custom work and retail sales only)................. | 1.25 | 1.75 |
| Hat and Cap Factories................ | 1.50 | 2.50 |
| *Hat and Cap Stocks, wholesale, no heating irons used........................ | 1.25 | 1.75 |
| *Hat and Cap Stocks, retail............. | 1.35 | 1.85 |
| Hay in Stacks ........................ | | 6.00 |
| Hay Barns........................... | 2.50 | 4.50 |
| Hay Presses, horse power, in use........ | 2.00 | 3.50 |
| Hay Presses, steam power, in use†....... | 3.00 | 5.00 |
| Hemp in bales ....................... | 1.50 | 2.50 |
| Hide and Leather Stocks, no Findings..... | 1.00 | 1.50 |
| Hoisting Works, water power........... | 2.00 | 2.50 |
| Hoisting Works, steam power†.......... | 2.50 | 3.00 |
| Hops (see Brewers' Stocks)............. | 1.25 | 1.75 |

Hops, while contained in kilns, warehouses or other buildings where drying is done, may be written at basis rate of

The *basis rate* for C Class is one-fifth more than B Class.
†The charge for Steam Boiler or Steam Power is included.
‖See rule for Long Term Risks on page 35.

|  | B Class. | D Class. |
|---|---|---|

"Hops" with the following additional charge for drying privilege:

  B class .................................. .90
  D class .................................. 1.25

  The following form of permit is to be used: "Permitted to dry hops while contained in above described building."

  HOP KILNS may be written at "Hops" rate, with the charge for drying privilege added. This charge for drying covers one season only, and no deduction is to be made for shortness of term. Barns and other buildings temporarily used for the storage and drying of hops may retain their proper basis rate as barns, warehouses, etc., with drying charge added; but notice must be given and extra charge made.

| | B Class. | D Class. |
|---|---|---|
| Horse Collar Factories................. | 2.25 | 3.25 |
| Hospitals ‖.............................. | 1.25 | 2.00 |
| Hotels (see rules 6 and 18, pages 33 and 36; also see Frescoed Work)............... | 1.50 | 2.75 |
| * House Furnishing Goods.............. | 1.25 | 1.75 |
| Houses of Refuge and Reform Schools (to be specially rated).................. | | |
| | | |
| Ice Factories (to be specially rated)..... | | |
| Ice Houses and Stables belonging thereto... | 1.50 | 2.50 |
| India Rubber and Gutta Percha Stocks.... | 1.00 | 1.75 |
| Iron Stocks, without Shelf Goods.......... | 1.00 | 1.50 |
| | | |
| Jails, City and or County ‖................. | 1.00 | 1.75 |
| * Jewelry, Watch and Clock Stocks....... | 1.25 | 1.75 |

NOTE.—*The minimum rate for "Jewelry, Watch and Clock Stocks," when in iron safes, shall be one-fifth less than the rate of the same stock if outside of a safe in the store in which the safe is located.*

| | B Class. | D Class. |
|---|---|---|
| Jewelry Factories....................... | 1.25 | 2.00 |
| Junk and Rag Stocks.................... | 2.00 | 3.00 |
| Jute in bales.......................... | 1.50 | 2.50 |
| | | |
| * Lace and Embroidery Stocks........... | 1.35 | 2.00 |
| Ladies' and Children's Underwear Factories. | 1.25 | 2.00 |
| Lamp and Chandelier Stocks, without oils... | 1.25 | 2.00 |
| Last and or Hat Block Factories............. | 2.25 | 3.50 |

The *basis rate* for C Class is one-fifth more than B Class.
†The charge for Steam Boiler or Steam Power is included.
‖See rule for Long Term Risks on page 35.

| | B Class. | D Class. |
|---|---|---|
| Laundries, without drying-room (see Chinese Wash Houses)...................... | 1.50 | 2.50 |
| Laundries, with drying room †............ | 1.75 | 3.00 |
| Leasehold Interest, rates the same as the building......................... | | |
| Leather and Finding Stocks ............. | 1.25 | 1.75 |
| *Libraries, Public and Law............... | 1.25 | 1.75 |
| Lime, unslaked, and Cement (see Cement).. | 1.50 | 2.25 |
| Liquors, and or Wines, retail................. | 1.25 | 1.75 |
| Liquors, and or Wines, wholesale, without privilege of rectifying with fire heat (see note below)*............................. | 1.25 | 1.75 |
| Locomotives in Round Houses............ | 1.75 | 3.00 |
| Lodging Houses (see Boarding Houses).... | | |
| Looking Glass, Picture and Frame Stocks (no gilding or joining done)............ | 1.35 | 2.10 |
| Looking Glass, Picture and Frame Stocks (gilding or joining done)............... | 1.50 | 2.25 |
| Lumber Yards (see rules 6 and 7, pages 33 and 34, and rule 32, page 42).......... | | 1.50 |
| MACHINE SHOPS, without pattern shops †... | 2.00 | 3.50 |
| Machine Shops, with pattern shops † (see rule 31, page 42)....................... | 2.50 | 4.25 |
| Malt Houses †........................... | 3.25 | 4.75 |
| Manilla Grass in bales.................. | 1.50 | 2.50 |
| *Marble Yards and Shops............... | 1.25 | 2.00 |
| Market Houses......................... | 1.50 | 2.25 |
| Match Factories........................ | 3.25 | 5.00 |
| Mattress Factories and or Shops............. | 1.75 | 2.75 |
| Mechanics' Risk (see rules 8 and 9, page 34, and rule 16, page 36)................. | | |
| Melodeon Halls (see Theatres, etc.)....... | | |
| Merchant Tailors' Stocks, cutting and fitting only (see Tailors' Workrooms)......... | 1.00 | 1.50 |
| Milliners' Workrooms (see rule 2, page 32) | | |
| *Millinery Stocks....................... | 1.35 | 2.10 |

The *basis rate* for C Class is one-fifth more than B Class.
†The charge for Steam Boiler or Steam Power is included.
‖See rule for Long Term Risks on page 35.
*Reducing without the use of charcoal and coloring, not to be considered "Rectifying."

| | B<br>Class. | D<br>Class. |
|---|---|---|
| *Musical Instruments, and Sheet Music.... | 1.35 | 2.10 |
| Musical Instrument Factories, except organ,<br>   piano and melodeon................. | 1.50 | 2.50 |
| ................................... | ...... | .... |
| NAVAL STORES, Turpentine, Tar and Pitch. | 1.50 | 2.50 |
| Nitrate of Soda  (see rule 24, page 40).... | 1.25 | 1.75 |
| ................................... | ...... | ... |
| OAKUM in bales..................... | 1.50 | 2.50 |
| Offices, Law, Real Estate, Mining, etc...... | 1.00 | 1.50 |
| Oiled Clothing (suits to be hung five inches<br>   apart)........................... | 2.00 | 3.00 |
| Oil Stores and Stocks (see rule 19, page 37) | 2.00 | 3.00 |
| Opium, in bank vaults................. | .50 | ..... |
| *Optical and Mathematical Instruments and<br>   Shops........................... | 1.35 | 2.10 |
| Organ, Piano and Melodeon Factories, hand<br>   power .......................... | 2.25 | 3.50 |
| Outbuildings and Sheds ||............... | .75 | 1.00 |
| ................................... | ...... | ... |
| PAIL, BUCKET AND TUB FACTORIES, dry-<br>   house detached as per Tables of Exposures† | 5.00 | 8.00 |
| Pail, Bucket and Tub Factories, dry-house<br>   not detached † ...................... | 6.00 | 9.00 |
| Paint and Oil Stores.................. | 2.00 | 3.00 |
| Painters' Shops..................... | 1.70 | 3.00 |
| Paper Bag Factories, steam power †....... | 1.50 | 2.50 |
| Paper Box Factories.................. | 1.50 | 2.50 |
| *Paper Hanging Stocks................ | 1.25 | 2.00 |
| Paper Mills, water power.............. | 2.75 | 4.00 |
| Paper Mills, steam power †............. | 3.00 | 4.50 |
| *Paper Pattern Stocks................. | 1.50 | 2.50 |
| *Paper Stocks, in packages and reams..... | 1.25 | 2.00 |
| Patent Medicines.................... | 1.35 | 2.10 |
| Pattern Shops ...................... | 2.25 | 3.50 |
| *Pawnbrokers' Stocks................. | 1.75 | 2.75 |

The *basis rate* for C Class is one-fifth more than B Class.
†The charge for Steam Boiler or Steam Power is included.
||See rule for Long Term Risks on page 35.

[*Book San Fran.—2.]

|  | B Class. | D Class. |
|---|---|---|
| Penitentiaries, and Workshops in same (to be specially rated)...... |  |  |
| Perfumery Factories ...... | 1.50 | 2.25 |
| * Periodical and News Depots...... | 1.35 | 2.10 |
| Photograph Galleries, Furniture and Stock.. | 1.60 | 2.50 |
| Photograph Stocks, wholesale...... | 1.40 | 2.25 |
| Piano Forte Factories (see Organ Fact's).. |  |  |
| * Piano Stocks (see Musical Instruments).. | 1.35 | 2.10 |
| Pickle Factories †...... | 1.70 | 3.00 |
| Picture, Looking Glass and Frame Stocks (no gilding or joining done)...... | 1.35 | 2.10 |
| Picture, Looking Glass and Frame Stocks (gilding or joining done)...... | 1.50 | 2.25 |
| Planing and Grooving Mills, water power.. | 4.00 | 6.00 |
| Planing and Grooving Mills, steam power † | 6.00 | 9.00 |
| Plaster Mills †...... | 2.75 | 4.00 |
| * Plaster Ornament Shops...... | 1.50 | 2.50 |
| Plate Glass...... |  |  |

NOTE.—*For Plate Glass of the dimensions of 9 square feet or more, in buildings, charge 25 cents more than the rate of the building.*

| | B Class. | D Class. |
|---|---|---|
| Plow Factories, water or hand power...... | 2.00 | 3.00 |
| Plow Factories, steam power †...... | 2.25 | 3.50 |
| Plumbers', Gasfitters' and Bell Hangers' Stocks and Shops...... | 1.25 | 2.00 |
| Potteries...... | 2.50 | 3.50 |
| Powder Mills...... |  |  |
| Printing Offices, hand power...... | 1.50 | 2.25 |
| Printing Offices, steam power †...... | 1.75 | 2.75 |
| Produce and Provision Stores...... | 1.00 | 1.50 |

| | B Class. | D Class. |
|---|---|---|
| QUARTZ MILLS, water power...... | 2.00 | 2.50 |
| Quartz Mills, steam power †...... | 2.50 | 3.00 |
| Mill in operation, add for Roasting and or Dry Kiln process (B or C Class, 25)...... | .25 | .50 |
| Quicksilver works (B, C or D Class...... |  | 4.00 |

The *basis rate* for C Class is one-fifth more than B Class.
† The charge for Steam Boiler or Steam Power is included.
‖ See rule for Long Term Risks on page 35.

|  | B Class. | D Class. |
|---|---|---|
| Rag and Junk Stocks................... | 2.00 | 3.00 |
| Reduction and Smelting Works, steam power† | 2.75 | 3.50 |
| Reform Schools (to be specially rated)..... | | |
| *Regalia and Emblem Stocks, Masonic and other Orders......................... | 1.25 | 1.75 |
| Rents rate the same as the building........ | | |
| Restaurants and Eating Houses.......... | 1.50 | 2.50 |
| Roofing Material (Composition) without manufacturing...................... | 1.75 | 3.25 |
| Rope and Cordage Stocks............... | 1.25 | 2.00 |
| Rope Walks† .......................... | 3.00 | 4.50 |
| Round Houses......................... | 1.75 | 3.00 |
| *Ruffle and Ruche Factories. ............ | 1.50 | 2.50 |
| .......................................... | | |
| Saddle and Harness Factories (no collar making). .......................... | 1.50 | 2.50 |
| Saddle and Harness Factories (with collar making)............................ | 2.00 | 3.00 |
| *Saddle and Harness Stocks, wholesale..... | 1.25 | 1.75 |
| *Saddle and Harness Stocks (custom work and retail sales only) ................. | 1.25 | 1.75 |
| Sail, Awning and Tent Makers........... | 1.25 | 1.75 |
| Salmon Canning Establishments, with warranty that lacquer shall not be kept or used in main cannery building or within twenty feet thereof (see rules 26 & 27, pp. 40 & 41) | 2.75 | 3.00 |
| Salmon Canning Establishments, with permit for use of lacquer (see rules 26 and 27, pages 40 and 41)................. | 3.00 | 3.50 |
| Saloons and Sample Rooms (see rule 6, p. 33) | 1.25 | 1.75 |
| Salt Mills †............................ | 1.50 | 2.50 |
| Salt Stocks............................ | 1.00 | 1.75 |
| Saltpeer Stocks ....................... | 1.50 | 2.50 |
| Sash Factories (see Blinds and Doors)..... | | |
| Saw Mills, water power................. | 3.50 | 5.00 |
| Saw Mills, steam power †................ | 6.00 | 9.00 |

The *basis rate* for C Class is one-fifth more than B Class.
†The charge for Steam Boiler or Steam Power is included.
‖See rule for Long Term Risks on page 35.

| | B Class. | D Class. |
|---|---|---|
| Saw Mills, wet logs, water power.......... | | |
| Saw Mills, wet logs, steam power.......... | | |
| NOTE.—*Rates on wet log saw mills apply to mills, logs for which are stored exclusively in water, and which have no dry houses.* | | |
| School Houses, public and private, day schools only ‖.............................. | .75 | 1.25 |
| *Seed Stores........................... | 1.25 | 2.00 |
| Seminaries, day students only ‖............ | .75 | 1.25 |
| Seminaries, boarding, with dormitories ‖.... | .90 | 1.50 |
| *Sewing Machine Salesrooms............. | 1.10 | 1.65 |
| Shake Roofs (see rule 4, page 32)........ | | |
| Shingle Mills, water power............... | 4.00 | 6.00 |
| Shingle Mills, steam power............... | 6.00 | 9.00 |
| Ships in port, and laid up (wood or iron)... | | 1.50 |
| Ships on stocks (wood or iron)............ | | 2.00 |
| Ship Carpenters' and Joiners' Shops....... | 2.25 | 3.50 |
| Ship Chandlers' Stocks.................. | 1.50 | 2.50 |
| Shipsmiths' Shops...................... | 1.50 | 2.50 |
| Shirt Factories, without laundries........ | 1.25 | 1.75 |
| Shirt Factories, with laundries........... | 1.50 | 2.25 |
| Silverware Factories.................... | 1.25 | 2.00 |
| Slaughter Houses...................... | 2.00 | 3.00 |
| Smoke and Packing Houses (to be specially rated)............................... | | |
| Soap $^{and}_{or}$ Candle Factories, without still †.... | 3.50 | 5.00 |
| Soap $^{and}_{or}$ Candle Factories, with still †...... | 4.00 | 6.00 |
| Soap Stocks (no manufacturing).......... | 1.00 | 1.75 |
| Soda Water Factories .................. | 1.25 | 2.00 |
| Stables, private, within the corporate limits of town ‖............................. | .75 | 1.00 |
| Stables, private, outside the corporate limits of town ‖............................. | | |
| Stables, private, outside of corporate limits of towns‖. If located within 100 yards of dwelling upon same premises on which stable is located...................... | | |
| Stables, Draymen's, Expressmen's $^{and}_{or}$ Contractor's, with not more than two horses .. | .75 | 1.00 |

The *basis rate* for C Class is one-fifth more than B Class.
†The charge for Steam Boiler or Steam Power is included
‖See rule for Long Term Risks on page 35.

| | B Class. | D Class. |
|---|---|---|
| Stables, Draymen's, Expressmen's **and or** Contractor's, having 3 and not more than 6 horses . . . . . . . . . . . . . . . . . . . . . . . . . . . . . | 1.25 | 2.00 |
| Stables, Draymen's, Expressmen's **and or** Contractor's, having more than 6 horses. . . . . . | 1.50 | 2.50 |
| Stables, Dairy. . . . . . . . . . . . . . . . . . . . . . . . | 1.50 | 2.50 |
| Stables, Hack, Omnibus and Car. . . . . . . . . . | 1.75 | 2.75 |
| Stables, Hotel. . . . . . . . . . . . . . . . . . . . . . . . | 1.75 | 2.75 |
| Stables, Livery **and or** Boarding . . . . . . . . . . . . | 2.25 | 3.50 |
| Stave Yards (see rules 6 and 7, pp. 33 and 34) | | 1.50 |
| Steamboats on stocks or laid up. . . . . . . . . . | | 2.00 |
| Steamboats, while running. . . . . . . . . . . . . . | | 2.50 |
| Stoves and Hollow-ware (no Tin Shop) . . . . | 1.00 | 1.50 |
| Stoves and Hollow-ware, with Tin Shop. . . . | 1.25 | 1.75 |
| . . . . . . . . . . . . . . . . . . . . . . . . . . . . . . . . . . . . | . . . . | . . . . |
| TAILORS' Work-rooms (see rule 2, page 32). | 1.10 | 1.85 |
| Tank-frames (not inclosed), together with tanks and windmills thereon ‖ . . . . . . . . . | | .60 |
| Tank-houses (inclosed), together with tanks and windmills thereon ‖ . . . . . . . . . . . . . . | | 1.00 |
| Tanneries (no steam power). . . . . . . . . . . . . | 3.25 | 4.25 |
| Tanneries, steam power † . . . . . . . . . . . . . . . | 3.75 | 5.00 |
| Theaters and Melodeons. . . . . . . . . . . . . . . . | 4.50 | 7.50 |
| Theaters and Melodeons—Stocks on ground floor, charge two-thirds of Theatre rates without regard to class of stocks. . . . . . . . . | | |
| Tin Shops and Sheet-Iron Workers. . . . . . . . | 1.25 | 1.75 |
| Toll Houses . . . . . . . . . . . . . . . . . . . . . . . . . | .75 | 1.00 |
| Toy Stocks. . . . . . . . . . . . . . . . . . . . . . . . . . | 1.35 | 2.25 |
| Trunk Factories, hand power. . . . . . . . . . . . | 2.25 | 3.50 |
| Trunk Factories, steam power † . . . . . . . . . . | 6.00 | 9.00 |
| Trunk Stocks. . . . . . . . . . . . . . . . . . . . . . . . . | 1.25 | 1.75 |
| Turners in Wood, hand or water power. . . . | 2.25 | 3.50 |
| Turners in Wood, steam power † . . . . . . . . . | 6.00 | 9.00 |
| Type Foundries. . . . . . . . . . . . . . . . . . . . . . . | 1.75 | 2.75 |
| *Type Stocks . . . . . . . . . . . . . . . . . . . . . . . . | 1.25 | 2.00 |
| . . . . . . . . . . . . . . . . . . . . . . . . . . . . . . . . . . . . | . . . . | . . . . |

The *basis rate* for C Class is one-fifth more than B Class.
†The charge for Steam Boiler or Steam Power is included.
‖See rule for Long Term Risks on page 35.

|  | B Class. | D Class. |
|---|---|---|
| UMBRELLA, Parasol and Cane Factories.... | 1.25 | 2.00 |
| Undertakers' Stocks (no manufacturing; see Coffin-makers' Shops)................. | 1.25 | 2.00 |
| Upholstery Factories.................... | 1.75 | 2.75 |
| Upholstery Stocks (no manufacturing)..... | 1.35 | 2.00 |
| .......................... | ...... | ..... |
| *VARIETY Stocks and Fancy Goods...... | 1.35 | 2.00 |
| Veneering and Molding Salesrooms........ | 1.50 | 2.25 |
| Vinegar Factories...................... | 1.70 | 3.00 |
| .......................... | ...... | ..... |
| WAGON MAKERS' SHOP................ | 2.00 | 3.00 |
| Wagons and Wagon Materials........... | 1.25 | 1.75 |
| *Wall Paper Stocks .................... | 1.25 | 2.00 |
| Warehouses, grain, bags, flour, beans, peas, lentils and seeds only................ | .75 | 1.25 |
| NOTE.—*Baled Hops may be stored in any D Class grain warehouse without increasing the rate on the other contents or on the building.* *The Baled Hops take their proper basis rate.* NOTE.—*For grain in bulk add to the above basis rates on the grain only, and not on the building (see Elevators, Grain, etc.* WOOL *may be insured in grain warehouses at the same rate as the grain and without increasing the rates of said warehouses.* | .25 | .50 |
| Warehouses, grain in bags and bags only, when the building exceeds two stories in height, to be specially rated........... |  |  |
| Warehouses, public (see page 23)........ |  |  |
| Warehouses, general storage (no broom-corn, hay, jute or oil—see rule 24, page 40)... | .90 | 1.75 |
| Warehouses, with storage of broom-corn and or jute...................... | 1.50 | 2.50 |
| Warehouses, with storage of oils.......... | 2.00 | 3.00 |
| Warehouses for Hay or Hay Barns........ | 2.50 | 4.50 |
| *Watchmakers' Stocks and Tools......... | 1.25 | 1.75 |
| Wharves, without roof................. |  | 1.50 |
| Wheelwrights' Shops................... | 2.00 | 3.00 |
| *Wig-Makers' Stocks.................. | 1.50 | 2.50 |

The *basis rate* for C Class is one-fifth more than B Class.
†The Charge for Steam Boiler or Steam Power is included.
‖See rule for Long Term Risks on page 35.

| | B Class. | D Class. |
|---|---|---|
| Willow-ware Factories................. | 1.40 | 2.25 |
| Wine Factories or Cellars (charge half per cent additional per month for privilege of distilling) ..................... | 1.10 | 1.50 |

NOTE.—*A permit for this privilege must be granted for a definite period, and the prescribed charge of one-half of one per cent per month collected in advance; no allowance or rebate may be made for lost time, or any extension of time or permit granted in lieu thereof. The charge applies to the building containing the still, and to all other buildings within thirty feet thereof, together with their contents.*

| | B Class. | D Class. |
|---|---|---|
| Wine and or Liquors (see Liquors)........... | | |
| Wine Stocks (no liquors, spirits or botling).................................. | 1.00 | 1.65 |
| *Wireworkers' Stocks (no manufacturing).. | 1.35 | 1.85 |
| Wood and or Coal Yards (see rules 6 and 7, page 33).................................. | | 1.75 |
| Wood and Willow-ware Stocks........... | 1.25 | 2.00 |
| Wool and Hide Stocks................. | 1.00 | 1.50 |
| Wool Pulling Establishments (to be specially rated).................................. | | |
| Wool Washing Shops†.................. | 1.50 | 2.25 |
| Woolen Mills (to be specially rated)...... | | |
| | | |
| YEAST POWDER FACTORIES............. | 1.50 | 2.50 |

The *basis rate* for C Class is one-fifth more than B Class.
†The charge for Steam Boiler or Steam Power is included.
║See rule for Long Term Risks on page 35.

## Public Warehouses.

[See Rule 24, "Chemicals," on page 40.]

All brick or stone Warehouses, used for general storage, no broom
corn, hay, jute or oil to be kept in the Warehouse, to rate at..$ .90
All brick or stone Warehouses, used for general storage, including broom corn and/or jute, to rate at .............. 1.50
All brick or stone Warehouses, used ONLY for general storage
of Wool and Hides, to rate at....................... .90
*All brick or stone Warehouses, used ONLY for general storage
of Grain, Bags, Flour, Beans, Peas, Lentils and Seeds, to rate at .75
All brick or stone Warehouses, in which are stored Coal Oil, or
the products of Earth Oil, to rate at.................... 2.00

* Baled Hops may be stored in any brick or stone Grain Warehouse without increasing the rate on the other contents or the building. The rate on Baled Hops in such Warehouse shall be 90 cents.

☞ Charges for *Deficiencies, Privileges* and *Exposures,* to be added (when they exist) to the *Basis Rate.*

---

# ADD TO B CLASS.

## PARTITIONS.

In a block or building of B Class, having ground floor* compartments for occupancy, each provided with an entrance from the street, and separated from each other by one or more ordinary boarded or studded and lathed and plastered partitions, to the *basis rate* of building and contents add 10 cents for each of such ground-floor partitions (see note to rule 8, page 34) which separates one occupancy from another.

*NOTE.—The ground-floor of a building shall be the first floor above the basement or cellar, or, if there be no basement or cellar, the floor nearest to the grade of the street upon which the building fronts.

## STOVE-PIPES AND EARTHEN-WARE CHIMNEYS.

For one or more Stove-pipes, Artificial Stone, Cement or Earthen-ware Chimneys, passing through a window or roof, to the *basis rate* of building and contents, add as follows, viz:

For one or more Stove-pipes.................................................. 25 cts.
For one or more Artificial Stone, Cement or Earthen-ware Chimneys..... 10 cts.

NOTE.—When a charge has to be made for a Stove-pipe, according to this rule, the charge for Artificial Stone, Cement or Earthen-ware Chimneys need not be added.

## STEAM BOILER OR STEAM POWER.

For Steam Boiler in the building, or for Steam Power in the building when the steam is generated either in the building or in another building situated within 20 feet thereof, to the *basis rate* of building and contents, (except when marked with a † in the "Alphabetical Table of Hazards"), add (see rule 21 page 39) 25 cts.

NOTE.—When the steam is generated in another building situated at a distance of 20 feet or more from the building to be rated, a deduction of 25 cents may be made from all B Class basis rates marked with a †.

## GASOLINE AND PETROLEUM STOVES.

For the use of Gasoline and/or Petroleum stoves, to the *basis rate* of building and contents (see rule 19, page 37) add as follows, viz :

For each Gasoline Stove................................................... 10 cts
For each Oil Stove to burn any product of petroleum which emits an inflammable vapor at less than 110° Fahrenheit without the medium of a wick. 10 cts.

## COAL OIL.

### PERMIT FOR COAL OIL IN A RETAIL STORE.

A permit may be granted to keep in a retail store 200 gallons of Refined Kerosene Oil, without charge. For each additional 100 gallons of Kerosene Oil kept in such a store, add 10 cents to the *basis rate* for building and contents. (See rules 16, page 36, and 19, page 37.)

### PERMIT FOR COAL OIL IN A WHOLESALE STORE.

A permit may be granted to keep in a wholesale store 1,000 gallons of Refined Kerosene Oil without charge. Such permits shall be in the following form, viz: "Permission is hereby granted the assured to keep in store an amount not exceeding 1,000 gallons of Refined Kerosene Oil in tin cans in unbroken packages. Packages of Kerosene Oil may be repacked, but re-filling or repairing of cans is hereby prohibited, unless consent therefor is endorsed hereon and the prescribed additional premium paid."

NOTE.—Re-filling or repairing of cans subjects the risk to the charge for keeping Kerosene Oil in retail stores.

## POWDER.

A permit may be granted to keep in store an amount not exceeding 50 pounds of Powder in metal cans, near the door, without charge. (See rule 25, page 40.)

CHARGES CONTINUED.

# ADD TO B CLASS.

## TABLE OF EXPOSURES.

To the *basis rate* of building and contents, add for such exposure within 40 feet in any direction, for which the *highest* additional rate is prescribed in the following Table. B or C Class buildings (except Mills, Factories, etc.) † are not to be regarded as exposures. (See rules 1 and 3, page 32; 6, page 33; and 14, page 36.)

| EXPOSURES FOR WHICH AN ADDITIONAL CHARGE IS TO BE ADDED TO THE *Basis Rate.* | ADDITIONS FOR THE SEVERAL DISTANCES. | | | |
|---|---|---|---|---|
| | Adj. to 10 ft. | 10 to 20 feet. | 20 to 30 feet. | 30 to 40 feet. |
| If a D Class Dwelling, Boarding-house, Church, Grain Warehouse, Office Buildsng, School-house, Private Stable or Barn......... | 5 cts. | | | |
| If a D Class Store, Mixed Occupancy,* Lumber, Wood or Coal Yard...... | 10 cts. | 5 cts. | | |
| If a D Class Boiler, Carpenter, Cooper, Machine or Wagon Shop, Brewery, Foundry, Hotel, Laundry, or Wash-house, Oil Warehouse, Hack, Omnibus, Car, Hotel or Livery Stable, water power Factory or Mill............... | 15 cts. | 15 cts. | 10 cts. | 5 cts. |
| If a D Class Warehouse for Hay, or Tannery; † B, C or D Class steam power Factory or Mill, *other than steam power Blind, Box, Door, Furniture, Pail or Sash Factory, Planing or Saw-mill, or Distillery*..... | 40 cts. | 40 cts. | 25 cts. | 15 cts. |
| If a D Class Theatre; † B, C or D Class steam power Blind, Box, Door, Furniture, Pail or Sash Factory, Planing or Saw-mill, or Distillery.............. | 100 cts. | 100 cts. | 75 cts. | 50 cts. |

☞ * Any building not otherwise specified, shall be treated as a Store or Mixed Occupancy.

☞ Charges for *Deficiencies, Privileges* and *Exposures*, to be added (when they exist) to the *Basis Rate.*

---

# ADD TO C CLASS.

## PARTITIONS.

In a block or building of C Class, having ground floor* compartments for occupancy, each provided with an entrance from the street, and separated from each other by one or more ordinary boarded or studded and lathed and plastered partitions, to the *basis rate* of building and contents add 10 cents for each of such ground-floor partitions (see note to rule 8, page 34) which separates one occupancy from another.

* NOTE.—The ground-floor of a building shall be the first floor above the basement or cellar, or, if there be no basement or cellar, the floor nearest to the grade of the street upon which the building fronts.

## STOVE-PIPES AND EARTHEN-WARE CHIMNEYS.

For one or more Stove-pipes, Artificial Stone, Cement or Earthen-ware Chimneys, passing through a window or roof, to the *basis rate* of building and contents, add as follows, viz:

For one or more Stove-pipes .......................................... 25 cts.
For one or more Artificial Stone, Cement or Earthen-ware Chimneys..... 10 cts.

NOTE.— *When a charge has to be made for a Stove-pipe according to this rule, the charge for an Artificial Stone, Cement or Earthen-ware Chimney need not be added.*

## STEAM BOILER OR STEAM POWER.

For Steam Boiler in the building, or for Steam Power in the building when the steam is generated either in the building or in another building situated within 20 feet thereof, to the *basis rate* of building and contents, (except when marked with a † in the "Alphabetical Table of Hazards") add (see rule 21, page 39), 25 cts.

NOTE.—When the steam is generated in another building situated at a distance of 20 feet or more from the building to be rated, a deduction of 25 cents may be made from all B Class basis rates marked with a †.

## GASOLINE AND PETROLEUM STOVES.

For the use of Gasoline and/or Petroleum Stoves, to the *basis rate* of building and contents (see rule 19, page 37) add as follows, viz:

For each Gasoline Stove....................... ..................... 10 cts.
For each Oil Stove to burn any product of petroleum which emits an inflammable vapor at less than 110° Fahrenheit without the medium of a wick. 10 cts.

## COAL OIL.

### PERMIT FOR COAL OIL IN A RETAIL STORE.

A permit may be granted to keep in a retail store 200 gallons of Refined Kerosene Oil, without charge. For each additional 100 gallons of Kerosene Oil kept in such a store, add 10 cents to the *basis rate* for building and contents. (See rules 16, page 36, and 19, page 37.)

### PERMIT FOR COAL OIL IN A WHOLESALE STORE.

A permit may be granted to keep in a wholesale store 1,000 gallons of Refined Kerosene Oil without charge. Such permits shall be in the following form, viz: "Permission is hereby granted the assured to keep in store an amount not exceeding 1,000 gallons of Refined Kerosene Oil in tin cans in unbroken packages. Packages of Kerosene Oil may be repacked, but re-filling or repairing of cans is hereby prohibited, unless consent therefor is endorsed hereon and the prescribed additional premium paid."

NOTE.—Re-filling or repairing of cans subjects the risk to the charge for keeping Kerosene Oil in retail stores.

## POWDER.

A permit may be granted to keep in store an amount not exceeding 50 pounds of Powder in metal cans, near the door, without charge. (See rule 25 page 40.)

CHARGES CONTINUED.

# ADD TO C CLASS.

## TABLE OF EXPOSURES.

To the *basis rate* of building and contents add for such **exposure** within 50 feet in any direction, for which the *highest* additional rate is prescribed in the following Table. B or C Class buildings (except Mills, Factories, etc.)† are not to be regarded as exposures. (See rules 1 and 3, page 32; 6, page 33; and 14, page 36.)

| EXPOSURES FOR WHICH AN ADDITIONAL CHARGE IS TO BE ADDED TO THE *basis rate*. | ADDITIONS FOR THE SEVERAL DISTANCES. | | | | |
|---|---|---|---|---|---|
| | Adj. to 10 ft. | 10 to 20 feet. | 20 to 30 feet. | 30 to 40 feet. | 40 to 50 feet. |
| If a D Class Dwelling, Boarding-House, Church, Grain Warehouse, Office Building, School House, Private Stable or Barn............ | 10 cts. | 5 cts. | | | |
| If a D Class Store, Mixed Occupancy,* Lumber, Wood or Coal Yard....... | 15 cts. | 10 cts. | 5 cts. | | |
| If a D Class Boiler, Carpenter, Cooper, Machine or Wagon Shop, Brewery, Foundry, Hotel, Laundry, or Wash-House, Oil Warehouse, Hack, Omnibus, Car, Hotel, or Livery Stable, water-power Factory or Mill................. | 25 cts. | 20 cts. | 15 cts. | 10 cts. | 5 cts. |
| If a D Class Warehouse for Hay, or Tannery; †B, C or D Class steam power Factory or Mill, *other than steam power Blind, Box, Door, Furniture, Pail, or Sash Factory, Planing or Saw Mill, or Distillery*..... | 60 cts. | 60 cts. | 40 cts. | 25 cts. | 15 cts. |
| If a D Class Theatre; †B, C or D Class steam power Blind, Box, Door, Furniture, Pail or Sash Factory, Planing or Saw Mill, or Distillery ............... | 125 cts | 125 cts | 100 cts | 75 cts. | 50 cts. |

☞ * Any building not otherwise specified, shall be treated as a Store or Mixed Occupancy.

☞ Charges for *Deficiencies, Privileges* and *Exposures*, to be added (when they exist) to the *Basis Rate*.

---

# ADD TO D CLASS.

## SINGLE D CLASS BUILDING.

### CLOTH LINING.

For *Cloth Lining* in the whole or in any part of a D Class Building, add as follows, viz:

To the *basis rate* of a D Class Dwelling and contents......................... 25 cts.
To the *basis rate* of any other D Class Building and contents............. 50 cts.

NOTE.—See rule 5, page 33.

### STOVE-PIPES AND EARTHEN-WARE CHIMNEYS.

For one or more Stove-pipes, Artificial Stone, Cement or Earthen-ware Chimneys, passing through a wall, window or roof of a D Class Dwelling or other D Class Building, to the *basis rate* of building and contents, add as follows:

For one or more Stove-pipes............................................. 25 cts.
For one or more Artificial Stone, Cement or Earthen-ware Chimneys.... 10 cts.

NOTE.—*When a charge has to be made for a Stove-pipe, according to this rule, the charge for an Artificial Stone, Cement or Earthen-ware Chimney need not be added.*

### STEAM BOILER OR STEAM POWER.

For Steam Boiler in the building, or for Steam Power in the building when the steam is generated either in the building or in another building situated within 20 feet thereof, to the *basis rate* of building and contents (except when marked with a † in the "Alphabetical Table of Hazards") add (see rule 21, page 39), 50 cts.

NOTE.—When the steam is generated in another building situated at a distance of 20 feet or more from the building to be rated, a deduction of 50 cents may be made from all D Class basis rates marked with a †.

### GASOLINE AND PETROLEUM STOVES.

For the use of Gasoline and/or Petroleum Stoves, to the *basis rate* of building and contents (see rule 19, page 37) add as follows, viz:

For each Gasoline Stove................................................. 10 cts.
For each Oil Stove to burn any product of petroleum which emits an inflammable vapor at less than 110° Fahrenheit without the medium of a wick.. 10 cts.

### COAL OIL.

#### PERMIT FOR COAL OIL IN A RETAIL STORE.

A permit may be granted to keep in a retail store 200 gallons of Refined Kerosene Oil, without charge. For each additional 100 gallons of Kerosene Oil kept in such a store, add 10 cents to the *basis rate* for building and contents. (See rules 16, page 36, and 19, page 37.)

#### PERMIT FOR COAL OIL IN A WHOLESALE STORE.

A permit may be granted to keep in a wholesale store 1,000 gallons of Refined Kerosene Oil without charge. Such permits shall be in the following form, viz: "Permission is hereby granted the assured to keep in store an amount not exceeding 1,000 gallons of Refined Kerosene Oil in tin cans in unbroken packages. Packages of Kerosene Oil may be repacked, but re-filling or repairing of cans is hereby prohibited, unless consent therefor is endorsed hereon and the prescribed additional premium paid.

NOTE.—Re-filling or repairing of cans subjects the risk to the charge for keeping Kerosene Oil in retail stores.

### POWDER.

A permit may be granted to keep in store an amount not exceeding 50 pounds of powder in metal cans, near the door without charge. (See rule 25, page 40.)

CHARGES CONTINUED.

# ADD TO D CLASS.

SINGLE D CLASS BUILDING not exposed within 10 feet.

### TABLE OF EXPOSURES.

To the *basis rate* of building and contents add for such exposure within 100 feet in any direction, for which the *highest* additional rate is prescribed in the following Table. B or C Class buildings (except Mills, Factories, etc.) † are not to be regarded as exposures.

*This Table applies only to a single D Class Building when not exposed within ten feet by other D Class Buildings.* (See rules 1 and 3, page 32; 6, page 33; and 14, page 36:)

| EXPOSURES FOR WHICH AN ADDITIONAL CHARGE IS TO BE ADDED TO THE *Basis Rate.* | ADDITIONS FOR THE SEVERAL DISTANCES. | | | | |
|---|---|---|---|---|---|
| | 10 to 25 feet. | 25 to 40 feet. | 40 to 60 feet. | 60 to 80 feet. | 80 to 100 feet. |
| If a D Class Dwelling, Boarding-house, Church, Grain Warehouse, Office Building, School-house, Private Stable or Barn.................... | 5 cts. | | | | |
| If a D Class Store, Mixed Occupancy,* Lumber, Wood or Coal Yard .............. | 25 cts. | 10 cts. | 5 cts. | | |
| If a D Class Boiler, Carpenter, Cooper, Machine or Wagon Shop, Brewery, Foundry, Hotel, Laundry or Washhouse, Oil Warehouse, Hack, Omnibus, Car, Hotel or Livery Stable, water power Factory or Mill.......... | 40 cts. | 20 cts. | 10 cts. | 5 cts. | |
| If a D Class Warehouse for Hay, or Tannery; † B, C or D Class steam power Factory or Mill, *other than steam power Blind, Box, Door, Furniture, Pail or Sash Factory, Planing or Saw-mill, or Distillery.*................... | 125 cts. | 100 cts. | 75 cts. | 30 cts. | 15 cts. |
| If a D Class Theatre; † B, C or D Class steam power Blind, Box, Door, Furniture, Pail or Sash Factory, Planing or Saw-mill, or Distillery..... | 275 cts. | 225 cts. | 175 cts. | 130 cts. | 50 cts. |

☞ *Any building not otherwise specified, shall be treated as a Store or Mixed Occupancy.

☞ Charges for *Deficiencies*, *Privileges* and *Exposures*, to be added (when they exist) to the *Basis Rate*.

---

# ADD TO D CLASS.

## D CLASS RANGE.*

### CLOTH LINING.

For *Cloth Lining* in the whole or in any part of a D Class Building, add as follows, viz :

To the *basis rate* of a D Class Dwelling and contents...................... 25 cts.
To the *basis rate* of any other D Class Building and contents............. 50 cts.

NOTE.—See rule 5, page 33.

### STOVE-PIPE AND EARTHEN-WARE CHIMNEYS.

For one or more Stove-pipes, Artificial Stone, Cement or Earthen-ware Chimneys, passing through a wall, window or roof of a D Class Dwelling or other D Class Building, to the *basis rate* of building and contents, add as follows :

For one or more Stove-pipes..................................................... 25 cts.
For one or more Artificial Stone, Cement or Earthen-ware Chimneys.... 10 cts.

NOTE.—*When a charge has to be made for a Stove-pipe, according to this rule, the charge for an Artificial Stone, Cement or Earthen-ware Chimney need not be added.*

### STEAM BOILER OR STEAM POWER.

For Steam Boiler in the building, or for Steam Power in the building when the steam is generated either in the building or in another building situated within 20 feet thereof, to the *basis rate* of building and contents, (except when marked with a † in the "Alphabetical Table of Hazards") add (see rule 21, page 39), 50 cts.

NOTE.—When the steam is generated in another building situated at a distance of 20 feet or more from the building to be rated, a deduction of 50 cents may be made from all D Class basis rates marked with a †.

### GASOLINE AND PETROLEUM STOVES.

For the use of Gasoline and/or Petroleum Stoves, to the *basis rate* of building and contents (see rule 19, page 37) add as follows, viz:

For each Gasoline Stove ....................................................... 10 cts.
For each Oil Stove to burn any product of petroleum which emits an inflammable vapor at less than 110° Fahrenheit without the medium of a wick. 10 cts.

### COAL OIL.

#### PERMIT FOR COAL OIL IN A RETAIL STORE.

A permit may be granted to keep in a retail store 200 gallons of Refined Kerosene Oil, without charge. For each additional 100 gallons of Kerosene Oil kept in such a store, add 10 cents to the *basis rate* for building and contents. (See rules 16, page 36, and 19, page 37.)

#### PERMIT FOR COAL OIL IN A WHOLESALE STORE.

A permit may be granted to keep in a wholesale store 1,000 gallons of Refined Kerosene Oil without charge. Such permits shall be in the following form, viz: "Permission is hereby granted the assured to keep in store an amount not exceeding 1,000 gallons of Refined Kerosene Oil in tin cans in unbroken packages. Packages of Kerosene Oil may be repacked, but re-filling or repairing of cans in hereby prohibited, unless consent therefor is endorsed hereon and the prescribed additional premium paid."

NOTE.—Re-filling or repairing of cans subjects the risk to the charge for keeping Kerosene Oil in retail stores.

### POWDER.

A permit may be granted to keep in store an amount not exceeding 50 pounds of Powder in metal cans, near the door, without charge. (See rule 25, page 40.)

* In a Frame Range, the above charges are to be added only to the Basis Rate of the building to be insured, or containing the property to be insured.

CHARGES CONTINUED.

# ADD TO D CLASS.

## D CLASS RANGE.

Two or more D Class buildings constitute a Range when they adjoin each other, or when there is less than 10 feet space between them on the front, rear or either side. (See rules 3, page 32; 6, 7 and 8, pages 33 and 34; 14 and 15, page 36.)

### TABLE OF EXPOSURES.

First ascertain the proper *basis rate*, as per "Rule for Determining Rate of Premium" on page 4, and then to such *basis rate* of any D Class building and its contents in a range of D Class buildings, add for every other building in the range, as follows in the † Table of Exposures below.

*This Table applies only to a D Class Range.*

(See rules 1 and 3, page 32; 6, 7 and 8, pages 33 and 34; 14 and 15, page 36.)

| EXPOSURES FOR WHICH AN ADDITIONAL CHARGE IS TO BE ADDED TO THE *Basis Rate.* | If next building on either side. | If next but one on either side. | If next but two on either side. |
|---|---|---|---|
| For each D Class Dwelling, Boarding House, Church, Grain Warehouse, Office Building, School House, Private Stable or Barn.......................... | 10 cts. | 5 cts. | |
| For each D Class Store, Mixed Occupancy*, Lumber, Wood or Coal Yard.......................... | 30 cts. | 20 cts. | 10 cts. |
| For each D Class Boiler, Carpenter, Cooper, Machine or Wagon Shop, Brewery, Foundry, Hotel, Laundry, or Wash House, Oil Warehouse, Hack, Car, Omnibus, Hotel or Livery Stable, water power Factory or Mill.............................. | 60 cts. | 40 cts. | 20 cts. |
| A. For each D Class Warehouse for Hay, or Tannery; B, C or D Class steam power Factory or Mill, *other than Blind, Box, Door, Furniture, Pail or Sash Factory, Planing or Saw Mill, or Distillery*........ | 225 cts. | 175 cts. | 100 cts. |
| B. For each Class Theater; B, C or D Class steam power Blind, Box, Door, Furniture, Pail or Sash Factory, Planing or Saw Mill, or Distillery...... | 450 cts. | 350 cts. | 200 cts. |

NOTE.—If there is any one of the hazards named in Sections A and B, of the above Table of Exposures, situated 10 feet or more distant from a D Class range in any direction, to the above charges for exposures *add also* the charge for such exposure for which the *highest* additional rate is prescribed in the Table of Exposures on page 29.

† Under the above Table exposures need be counted only to such distances as will embrace three (3) buildings (see rule 7, page 34) so situated on each side of and/or directly or diagonally in the rear of a proposed risk as to be within 10 feet of any portion of any of the buildings forming the range in which the risk is located.

DEDUCTIONS ON DWELLINGS ONLY.

On dwellings only, 5 cents may be deducted from the tariff rate thus obtained if the risk is detached three (3) feet or more (measured in accordance with rule 14, page 36) on either side, or 10 cents if so detached on both sides; provided that the deduction shall not make the rate of any dwelling less than 70 cents.

### MAXIMUM RATE.

The maximum rate for all buildings not specially rated shall be 10 per cent.

*☞ Any building not otherwise specified shall be treated as a Store or Mixed Occupancy.

# General Rules.

## No. 1.—Dwelling Houses.

In rating a dwelling, an outbuilding (except a barn or stable), need not be considered as an exposure; but a D Class barn and or stable must be charged for as an exposure to a dwelling, and a D Class dwelling must be charged for as an exposure to a barn and or stable. Two or more barns, stables or outbuildings, however, belonging to the same premises, need not be charged for as exposures to each other.

## No. 2.—Dentists, Doctors, Dressmakers, Etc.

When a dwelling house which is principally occupied as such, is partly occupied for doctors' or dentists' offices, dressmakers', milliners' or tailors' workrooms, or for a cobbler's shop, it may retain the *basis rate* of a dwelling.

## No. 3.—Brick and Frame Buildings.

When insuring a brick, stone, iron, adobe or concrete building, which has a frame addition (below the roof), specify a separate amount on such addition and its contents; charging on the brick, stone, iron, adobe or concrete portion and contents, the proper B or C Class rate; and on the frame addition and contents, D Class rate. Such frame addition (when occupied by the same person or firm) need not be considered as an exposure to the main building according to the Tables of Exposures. Unless such specifications are made, charge the D Class rate on the whole risk.

*Provided*, however, that a frame structure of any kind (excepting skylights, cornices, balustrades, and shake roof as per following rule 4) attached to the roof of a brick, stone, iron, adobe or concrete building, shall reduce such building to C Class.

## No. 4.—Awnings and Shake Roofs.

A *Wooden Awning* affixed to any building, and a *Shake or other Wooden Roof* over a metal, slate, tile, brick or composition roof of a B or C Class building, shall not be covered by a policy issued on the building, unless specially insured. The rate for an Awning or a Shake or other Wooden Roof shall be six per cent, unless the building to which it is attached shall rate higher than six per cent, in which case it shall take the rate of the building.

# No. 5.—Cloth Lining.

The rule on pages 28 and 30 is to be understood as follows, viz: Whenever any part of a D class building, the *basis rate* for which is 2.50 per cent or more, has cloth fastened to boards in any way, or stretched across studding or joists on sides or on ceilings, papered or not papered, the building and its contents shall be subjected to the charge for cloth lining according to the tariff; but cloth lining on side-walls or partitions only, when closely stretched on boards, need not be charged for in other risks. In any D class building, however, cloth on any *ceiling* shall subject the building, together with its contents, to the cloth lining charge; but in dwelling houses cloth securely fastened to closely boarded ceilings and papered over need not be charged for.

☞ The charges printed on pages 28 and 30, Books of Rates, for cloth lining to D class buildings, are hereby made to apply also to adobe buildings, whether B or C class.

(San Fran., 1 and 2—Page 33.)

## No. 6.—Buildings Occupied for a Common Purpose.

When two or more buildings (*used for any of the purposes described in list\* below*), adjoining or adjacent, are occupied by the same person or firm for a common purpose, so that the buildings, although separated, virtually constitute a single hazard, they need not be charged for as exposures to each other; provided the highest *basis rate* of any of the buildings so adjoining or adjacent to each other is made the *basis rate* for each one of said buildings according to its class, whether B, C or D; otherwise, each building *taking its proper basis rate*, in accordance with the rule on page 4 for determining the rate of premium, must be subject to the charge for exposures as per the Tables of Exposures on pages 25, 27, 29 and 31.

\*Lumber yards, or coal and wood yards, and their respective offices and sheds.

Two or more warehouses, under the same management, for storage of the same class of property, and their offices.

Store and private warehouse.

A private warehouse which need not be charged for, according to this rule, as an exposure to the store in connection with which it is used, need not be charged for as an exposure to any other building.

Cluster of buildings, forming a mill or manufacturing establishment (it being understood that dwellings and barns, even if occupied in connection with such mill or manufacturing establishment, must be regarded as exposures thereto.)

Separate buildings, composing an academy or school.

Bars, billiard rooms and barber shops in hotels, and cigar stands in saloons, need not be considered as separate occupancies.

In case a B or C Class building is within ten feet of, or adjoins and communicates with, an addition or another building (whether B, C or D Class), both being occupied by one person or firm, and all directly or indirectly opposite or communicating openings are not provided with wooden doors two inches in thickness and covered with tin or galvanized iron, or with iron doors or shutters at least three-sixteenths of an inch in thickness, the highest rated occupancy in either, unless prefixed with a star [\*] (see rule on page 4), shall be the *basis rate* for both, according to their class, B, C or D.

Examples:—Baker's Stock, with Bakery adjoining; charge the rate for "Bakeries." Furniture Stock (no upholstering) with workroom adjoining; charge the rate for "Furniture Stocks, where upholstering or setting up is done."

# No. 7.—Frame Buildings with Compartments.

Each compartment for occupancy, on the ground-floor of a D Class building, having more than one such compartment, shall be rated as a separate building, if provided with a separate entrance from the street; but the highest basis rate for any occupancy in such D Class building under one roof, having two or more occupancies, shall be the *basis* rate for such building $^{and}_{or}$ all its contents. If a D Class building, having two or more such ground-floor compartments, be insured in a single sum, the rate therefor shall be that of the highest rated compartment of such building. This highest rate shall also be the rate for all the contents contained in two or more compartments of the building above the ground-floor, when such contents are insured in a single sum. A Lumber, Wood or Coal Yard shall be classed as a D Class building, and all the rules applying to a D Class building apply also to a Lumber, Wood or Coal Yard.

---

**Change Rule No. 8, Page 34.**

# No. 8.—Buildings in Course of Construction.

The rate for a building in course of construction shall be according to the Rule for Determining Rate of Premium on Page 4, —foot note†—

But it is provided that, it being warranted by the assured that the building shall not be occupied during the life of the Policy, the rate *may* be the basis rate of its Class, as per Classification of Buildings, page 5, with exposure charges added; but this does not annul any rule for rating frame ranges.

NOTE.—In rating these risks special attention is called to Rule 13, on page 36.

*Circular No. 33, Second Series.*

---

# No. 9.—Alterations and Repairs.

For alterations or repairs to a building, the following permit must be inserted in all policies covering on the building $^{and}_{or}$ its contents, viz:

### Permit.

"Privileged to make ordinary alterations and repairs, but it is understood that extraordinary alterations or repairs are prohibited, without notice to, and consent of, this Company, in writing."

NOTE.—For the privilege of making extraordinary alterations or repairs, or external additions to the premises, charge at the rate of ten cents a month for every day in excess of fifteen days.

# No. 10.—Buildings Being Removed.

A D Class building which has been removed, or is being removed to a new location, shall take the *Basis Rate* and charge or charges for exposures in that new location.

# No. 11.—Removal of Property.

In case of removal of property insured to another building, the difference in rate arising in consequence of such removal shall be collected *pro rata* for the unexpired term of the policy.

# No. 12.—Long Term Risks.

### DWELLING HOUSES.

Dwellings and their private barns, stables, out-buildings and/or their contents, and fences pertaining thereto, may be insured for two years at three-fifths more than the annual rate, for three years at twice the annual rate.

### OTHER BUILDINGS.

Academies, bridges, churches, colleges, hospitals, seminaries, school-houses and State, county, city or town public buildings and/or their contents, may be written for two years at three-fifths more than the annual rate, and for three years at twice the annual rate.

Farm dwellings and the private barns, stables, out-buildings and/or their contents, and fences pertaining thereto, when not subject to any charge for exposure by other than farm buildings, may be written for five years at not less than three times the annual premium thereon.

No property of any description shall be insured for a longer period than one year, except such buildings and their contents as are named in the above rule for Long Term Risks, and which come within the requirements of said rule.

## No. 13.—Short Term Risks.

A risk taken for a period less than one year, or canceled at the request of the assured, shall be charged for at the short rate of the annual rate, as per Short Rate Table, on page 43.

Note.—The suspension for a time of a policy in force is a violation of this rule. (See page 44.)

## No. 14.—Distances Between Buildings.

Distances between buildings shall be measured from the most contiguous points of the buildings, or of any sheds, privies, awnings, porches, piazzas, bay-windows, stairways or additions of any kind attached thereto, except roof cornices, open platforms or bridges.

## No. 15.—Intervening Brick Wall.

If a brick or stone building, or if a substantial brick or stone wall, (the latter without openings, and not less than twelve inches in thickness below the adjoining roof or roofs, and extending two feet above the adjoining roof or roofs) wholly intervenes between D Class buildings and all additions thereto, the exposure shall be counted therefrom.

## No. 16.—Permits and Privileges.

Any permit or privilege granted must be for a specific period, and the prescribed extra rate for the same (if any) must be charged in advance.

## No. 17.—Boarding and Lodging Houses.

A **Boarding** and (or) **Lodging House** is a building which is used for boarding and (or) lodging purposes by the day, week or month, without a saloon or bar therein, and containing ten or more furnished or unfurnished sleeping rooms, not including those actually used by the family of the proprietor.

## No. 18.—Hotels.

A **Hotel** is a public house for the accommodation of transient guests, and that has a bar or saloon in the building.

# No. 19.—Petroleum Products, and Gas Machines.

Decline, unconditionally, to give any permit for the use or storage of gasoline, or any of the products of petroleum, which emit an inflammable vapor at less than 110° Fahrenheit, for lighting, heating or cooking purposes in any building.

But the use of Portable Gasoline Stoves, and of Stoves to burn petroleum without wick, may be permitted, provided that the proper additional premium be paid (see pages 24, 26, 28 and 30), and the following warranty inserted.

## Portable Gasoline Stoves.

The following warranty must be inserted in all policies covering on buildings and contents where gasoline stoves are used, viz:

"Warranted by the assured that the reservoir is to be filled during daylight only, when the stove is not in use, and that no artificial light be permitted in the room when the reservoir is being filled; and no gasoline, except that contained in said reservoir, shall be kept within the building; and not more than five gallons, in a tight and entirely closed metallic can, free from leak, on the premises adjacent thereto."

## Petroleum Stoves without Wicks.

The following warranty must be inserted in all policies covering on buildings and contents where oil stoves are used to burn any product of petroleum which emits an inflammable vapor at less than 110° Fahrenheit without the medium of a wick, viz:

"Warranted by the assured that the tank or reservoir containing the oil be not less than twenty-five feet from the building."

### CAUTION.

The danger from Gasoline Stoves is not so much in themselves as in having the gasoline about. At ordinary temperature gasoline continually gives off inflammable vapor, and a light some distance from it will ignite it through the medium of this vapor. It is said that ONE PINT OF GASOLINE WILL IMPREGNATE 200 CUBIC FEET OF AIR and make it explosive; and it depends upon the proportion of air and vapor whether it becomes a burning gas or destructive explosive. Beware of any leaks in cans, and never forget how dangerous a material you are handling. Never attempt to fill the stove reservoir while the stove is burning, or if any other light is in the room. A little carelessness may hazard your LIFE as well as property.

## Gas Machines.

Permission for the use of a Gasoline Gas Machine may be granted, with the following express stipulation inserted in the Policy, viz:
"Warranted by the assured, that gasoline or gasoline material shall not be kept in, or taken into, the building insured, or the contents of which are insured under this Policy, and that the carburetter, generator and reservoir shall be located at least thirty feet from the said building."

# No. 20.—Writing of Policies.

**A.** A Blanket Policy, covering under one sum separate or distinct risks or items of hazard, is hereby prohibited.

**B.** A policy covering the contents of a dwelling shall be written to cover a specific amount on each item to be insured, in form, viz:

$......On household furniture, *useful and ornamental,* and
        family stores.
$......On family wearing apparel.
$......On printed books.
$......On silver and plated ware.
$......On pictures *and other works of art.*

NOTE.—The articles described in italics *need* not be included. None of the above items, other than those to be insured, need be mentioned in the policy.

**C.** A Policy on a Mercantile risk shall, in all cases, be written to cover a specific amount on Stock, and on Store Furniture and Fixtures.

**D.** A Policy on a Manufacturing risk shall, in all cases, be written to cover a specific amount on building—Engine and Boiler—Other Machinery, Tools and Fixtures—Stock manufactured, in process of manufacture, and material for manufacturing the same.

**E.** A Policy on a Printing, Lithographing or other similar establishment, shall be written to cover a specific amount on Engine and Boiler—on Printing Presses and other fixed and Movable Machinery, Implements, Tools, Furniture and Fixtures—on Type—on Lithographic Stones—on Stock and Supplies, and work finished and in process of completion.

In all policies covering such establishments, the following warranty shall be inserted: "It is warranted by the assured that no more than one gallon in all, of naphtha or benzine, shall be kept in the premises at any time."

## Specific Insurance on Each of Two or More Buildings.

**F.** Two or more brick buildings, separated by brick walls, with or without openings, must be separately insured, whether the walls rise above the roofs or not.

**G.** No policy shall cover, under one amount, two or more frame buildings, even if under the same roof, unless they are adjoining and communicating, *and are so described in the policy.*

## Contents of Separate Buildings.

**H.** The contents of two or more brick buildings, separated by walls, without openings, must be specifically insured.

**I.** The contents of two or more brick buildings, communicating with each other by openings, protected by fire doors, must be insured specifically, unless the co-insurance clause is made a part of the policy, and the rate re-adjusted.

**J.** The contents of two or more brick buildings, communicating by openings, unprotected by fire doors, may be insured under one sum, provided the rate for contents of the highest rated building shall be charged.

**K.** No policy shall cover, under one amount, the contents of two or more frame buildings, unless such buildings are adjoining and communicating, *and are so described in the policy.*

## Contents of Safes and Vaults.

**L.** The contents of an iron safe or of a vault, closed by good fire doors, may be insured at twenty per cent less than the rate of the stock of which they form a part. The contents of such safe or vault can be insured at forty per cent less than the rate of the stock of which they form a part, *if the co-insurance clause is made part of the policy.*

**M.** All Policies covering the same risk, written by members of this Union shall be made concurrent.

**N.** In case a policy has been irregularly or incorrectly written, by decision of a majority vote of the members of the Union present at a regular meeting, it shall be taken up and rewritten.

**O.** Permission for other insurance shall be given in the following words, to wit: "Permission for $——other insurance, concurrent herewith."

## No. 21.—Steam Boiler or Steam Power.

Whenever, in the Alphabetical Table of Hazards, a *basis rate* is prescribed for a hazard including a charge for a steam boiler or steam power, and no specific *basis rate* is prescribed for the same hazard without steam boiler or steam power, a deduction (25 cents from B and C Class, and 50 cents from D Class) may be made from the *basis rate* of the former to determine the *basis rate* of the latter.

The use of a Baxter engine and boiler, or Payne's Eureka boiler and engine, shall not necessitate the additional charge for steam power, and where the same only is used in risks, rates of which (*other than special rates*) include charge for steam power, a reduction of 25 cents from B and C Class, and 50 cents from D Class basis rate, may be made.

## No. 22.—General Merchandise Stock.

A General Merchandise Stock is one with which any *two or more* of the following kinds of goods are kept for sale *in connection with other stock having a basis rate not exceeding that of General Merchandise,* viz:

1. Agricultural Implements, Blinds, Sashes and Doors.
2. Books and Stationery.
3. Crockery, China and Glass-ware.
4. Drugs and Patent Medicines.
5. Furniture.
6. Groceries and Liquors.
7. Hardware, Stoves and Tin-ware.
8. Paints, Oil and Glass.
9. Toys and Variety Stocks.

## No. 23.—Boot and Shoe Factories.

The following conditions must be inserted in all policies covering on Boot and Shoe Factory buildings or their contents, viz:

"Warranted by the assured that no more than three quarts of Rubber Cement shall be kept in the factory, or in any building connected therewith, or within twenty feet thereof."

## No. 24.—Chemicals.

When any of the Chemicals named in the following list are stored in the Public Warehouses used for general storage, the rate of insurance on said warehouses and (or) their contents will be increased one-half of one per cent. per annum, whenever the fact that these articles are kept on storage shall come to the knowledge of the Union: Bi-Chloride of Tin, Bi-Sulphide of Carbon, Chlorate of Potash, and all other Chlorates, Ethers, Fulminates of Silver or Mercury, Metallic Potassium, Metallic Sodium, Methylic Alcohol, Nitrate of Ammonia, Nitrate of Potash, Nitrate of Soda, Nitro-Benzole, Phosphorus, Quicklime, Saltpeter, Sweet Spirits of Nitcr.

The rule prohibiting the storage of the above-named Chemicals in the public warehouses does not apply to such as are used exclusively for the storage of those articles, but only to such as are used for general storage.

## No. 25.—Powder.

The keeping of more than 50 pounds of powder in any store shall not be consented to by or on behalf of any Company represented in the Pacific Insurance Union.

NOTE.—When business requirements necessitate the keeping of larger quantities in stock, the excess should be stored in a magazine building, conspicuously marked "Powder." This magazine should be so remote from other buildings and main streets as not to jeopardize life or property.

It is urgently recommended that powder in stores be kept in an air-tight metallic box, to be also conspicuously marked "Powder," and stationed near an entrance to the building, so as to be easy of removal in the event of an alarm of fire.

## No. 26.—Fruit, Salmon or other Canning Establishments.

The following form of warranty must be inserted in ALL policies covering on Fruit, Salmon or other Canning Establishments and (or) their contents, viz:

"Warranted by the assured, that benzine, naphtha, or other product of petroleum (except refined kerosene oil for lighting purposes) shall not be kept or used on or in the premises, either for the reduction of lacquer or for any other purpose."

In addition to the above warranty one of the two following forms must also be inserted in all policies covering on Salmon Canning Establishments and (or) their contents, viz: The first form for such establishments in which lacquer is not kept or used, and the second form for such establishments in which lacquer is kept and used:

### FIRST FORM.

"Warranted by the assured that lacquer shall not be kept or used in the main cannery building or within twenty feet thereof."

### SECOND FORM.

"Permission is hereby granted to keep and use lacquer."

*Permission may be granted for the use of lacquer in Fruit and other Canning Establishments (except Salmon) without extra charge.*

## Stock in Fruit Canneries not in Operation.

*Stock* stored in fruit cannery buildings may be insured at general warehouse rates, the following warranty clause being made part of each policy covering same, viz:

"Warranted by the assured that no canning or packing of fruit shall be done in above described building during the life of this policy."

## No. 27.—Salmon Canning Establishments.

The *basis rate* for Salmon-Canning Establishments in the Alphabetical Table of Hazards, in the several Books of Rates, is intended to apply to those risks throughout the whole year, whether the establishments are in operation or not, and no return of premium can·be made on account of suspension of work.

## No. 28.—Electric Light.

The following form of permit may be given for the use of Electric Light, viz:

"Permission granted to use electric lights. Wires to be doubly coated with approved insulating material, and to have at least DOUBLE the conducting capacity required by the generators, and to be protected by porcelain or hard rubber insulators where they enter the building. Lamp frames to be insulated, and to have globes closed at the bottom, and at the top, by chimney with spark arresters where, ignitable materials are exposed."

## No. 29.—Watchman's Clause.

Form to be used whenever under the regulations of the Pacific Insurance Union, the watchman clause is required to be inserted in the policy :

" Warranted by the assured that at all times when the above Mill or Works shall be idle, or not in operation, one or more watchmen shall be kept constantly on duty, day and night, and if said Mill or Works are shut down for more than thirty days at any one time, notice shall be given this company, and permission to remain idle endorsed hereon, or this policy shall cease and determine."

## No. 30.—Opium and Treasure Clause.

The following clause must form a part of every policy covering the stock of a Chinese store :

" Opium, treasure, printed books, books of account, safe and contents, are not included in this insurance."

## No. 31. Patterns.

Machine shop and foundry patterns shall be insured specifically, and when the sum thereon shall exceed ten per cent of the amount of the policy, the co-insurance clause shall be added to this item of the policy.

## No. 32. Lumber Yards.

A deduction of twenty-five per cent of the established rate may be made, when the following clause forms part of a policy, covering a lumber yard:

Four-fifths Co-insurance Clause.—" It is a part of the consideration of this policy, and the basis upon which the rate of premium is fixed, that the assured shall maintain insurance on the property hereby insured by this policy, to the extent of four-fifths of the actual cash value thereof, and that failing so to do, the assured shall be a co-insurer to the extent of such deficit; and, in that event, shall bear his, her or their proportion of any loss. It is, however, mutually understood and agreed, that in case the total insurance shall exceed four-fifths of the whole actual cash value of the property insured by this policy, the assured shall not recover from this Company more than its *pro rata* share of four-fifths of the whole actual cash value of such property."

# Table of Short Rates for Terms less than a Year.

| ANNUAL PREMIUM. | CTS. 50 | CTS. 55 | CTS. 60 | CTS. 65 | CTS. 70 | CTS. 75 | CTS. 80 | CTS. 85 | CTS. 90 | CTS. 100 | CTS. 110 | CTS. 125 |
|---|---|---|---|---|---|---|---|---|---|---|---|---|
| 2 days or less........ | 2 | 2 | 2 | 2 | 2 | 3 | 3 | 3 | 3 | 3 | 4 | 4 |
| 5 days or less........ | 3 | 4 | 4 | 4 | 5 | 5 | 5 | 6 | 6 | 7 | 7 | 8 |
| 10 days or less........ | 5 | 6 | 6 | 7 | 7 | 8 | 8 | 9 | 9 | 10 | 11 | 13 |
| 15 days or less........ | 7 | 7 | 8 | 9 | 9 | 10 | 11 | 11 | 12 | 13 | 15 | 17 |
| 20 days or less........ | 8 | 9 | 10 | 11 | 12 | 13 | 13 | 14 | 15 | 17 | 18 | 21 |
| 1 month or less...... | 10 | 11 | 12 | 13 | 14 | 15 | 16 | 17 | 18 | 20 | 22 | 25 |
| 45 days or less....... | 14 | 15 | 17 | 18 | 19 | 21 | 22 | 23 | 25 | 28 | 30 | 34 |
| 2 months or less..... | 15 | 17 | 18 | 20 | 21 | 23 | 24 | 26 | 27 | 30 | 33 | 38 |
| 75 days or less........ | 19 | 21 | 23 | 24 | 26 | 28 | 30 | 32 | 34 | 38 | 41 | 47 |
| 3 months or less..... | 20 | 22 | 24 | 26 | 28 | 30 | 32 | 34 | 36 | 40 | 44 | 50 |
| 4 months or less..... | 25 | 28 | 30 | 33 | 35 | 38 | 40 | 43 | 45 | 50 | 55 | 63 |
| 5 months or less...... | 30 | 33 | 36 | 39 | 42 | 45 | 48 | 51 | 54 | 60 | 66 | 75 |
| 6 months or less...... | 35 | 39 | 42 | 46 | 49 | 53 | 56 | 60 | 63 | 70 | 77 | 88 |
| 7 months or less...... | 38 | 41 | 45 | 49 | 53 | 56 | 60 | 64 | 68 | 75 | 83 | 94 |
| 8 months or less...... | 40 | 44 | 48 | 52 | 56 | 60 | 64 | 68 | 72 | 80 | 88 | 1 00 |
| 9 months or less...... | 43 | 47 | 51 | 55 | 60 | 64 | 68 | 73 | 77 | 85 | 94 | 1 06 |
| 10 months or less...... | 45 | 50 | 54 | 59 | 63 | 68 | 72 | 77 | 81 | 90 | 99 | 1 13 |
| 11 months or less...... | 48 | 52 | 57 | 62 | 67 | 71 | 76 | 81 | 86 | 95 | 1 05 | 1 19 |

| ANNUAL PREMIUM. | CTS. 150 | CTS. 175 | CTS. 200 | CTS. 225 | CTS. 250 | CTS. 275 | CTS. 300 | CTS. 350 | CTS. 400 | CTS. 450 | CTS. 500 |
|---|---|---|---|---|---|---|---|---|---|---|---|
| 2 days or less............. | 5 | 6 | 7 | 8 | 8 | 9 | 10 | 12 | 13 | 15 | 17 |
| 5 days or less............. | 10 | 12 | 13 | 15 | 17 | 18 | 20 | 25 | 28 | 32 | 35 |
| 10 days or less............. | 15 | 18 | 20 | 23 | 25 | 28 | 30 | 35 | 40 | 45 | 50 |
| 15 days or less............. | 20 | 23 | 27 | 30 | 33 | 37 | 40 | 46 | 52 | 60 | 65 |
| 20 days or less............. | 25 | 29 | 33 | 38 | 42 | 46 | 50 | 60 | 68 | 77 | 85 |
| 1 month or less............. | 30 | 35 | 40 | 45 | 50 | 55 | 60 | 70 | 80 | 90 | 1 00 |
| 45 days or less............. | 41 | 48 | 55 | 62 | 69 | 76 | 83 | 98 | 1 12 | 1 26 | 1 40 |
| 2 months or less............. | 45 | 53 | 60 | 68 | 75 | 83 | 90 | 1 05 | 1 20 | 1 35 | 1 50 |
| 75 days or less............. | 56 | 66 | 75 | 85 | 94 | 1 03 | 1 13 | 1 33 | 1 52 | 1 71 | 1 90 |
| 3 months or less............. | 60 | 70 | 80 | 90 | 1 00 | 1 10 | 1 20 | 1 40 | 1 60 | 1 80 | 2 00 |
| 4 months or less............. | 75 | 88 | 1 00 | 1 13 | 1 25 | 1 38 | 1 50 | 1 75 | 2 00 | 2 25 | 2 50 |
| 5 months or less........ . | 90 | 1 05 | 1 20 | 1 35 | 1 50 | 1 65 | 1 80 | 2 10 | 2 40 | 2 70 | 3 00 |
| 6 months or less............. | 1 05 | 1 23 | 1 40 | 1 58 | 1 75 | 1 93 | 2 10 | 2 45 | 2 80 | 3 15 | 3 50 |
| 7 months or less............. | 1 13 | 1 31 | 1 50 | 1 69 | 1 88 | 2 06 | 2 25 | 2 63 | 3 00 | 3 38 | 3 75 |
| 8 months or less............. | 1 20 | 1 40 | 1 60 | 1 80 | 2 00 | 2 20 | 2 40 | 2 80 | 3 20 | 3 60 | 4 00 |
| 9 months or less........ . | 1 28 | 1 49 | 1 70 | 1 91 | 2 13 | 2 34 | 2 55 | 2 98 | 3 40 | 3 83 | 4 25 |
| 10 months or less............. | 1 35 | 1 58 | 1 80 | 2 03 | 2 25 | 2 48 | 2 70 | 3 15 | 3 60 | 4 05 | 4 50 |
| 11 months or less............. | 1 43 | 1 66 | 1 90 | 2 14 | 2 38 | 2 61 | 2 85 | 3 33 | 3 80 | 4 29 | 4 75 |

NOTE.—The rates per annum, from 50 cents to 500 cents (or 5 per cent.), are shown in the upper row of figures ; and the days below indicate the tariff from two days to eleven months.

# General Resolutions.

## Suspension of Policies.

The following resolution was adopted at a meeting of the Union:

*Resolved*, That the suspension for a time of a policy in force is a plain violation of Rule No. 13, for Short Term Risks, in the several Books of Rates.

The following resolution was unanimously passed at a meeting of the Union held July 14th, 1885:

*Resolved*, That on all days when the offices of the banking institutions of San Francisco shall be closed for a holiday, the offices of the members of the Pacific Insurance Union in San Francisco shall also be closed; and the Secretary hereby is authorized to give notice thereof in one morning and one evening daily newspaper published in San Francisco.

"All the risks which have been specially rated by the Pacific Insurance Union are subject to the rules for the additional charges for coal oil, and for the use of gasoline stoves, and petroleum stoves without wicks, as found on pages Nos. 24, 26, 28, and 30 of Book of Rates, applying to the locality of the risk."

www.ingramcontent.com/pod-product-compliance
Lightning Source LLC
Chambersburg PA
CBHW030909260626
47169CB00008B/2768